A special note from the author

Let me start by greeting you, the reader, by saying Namaskar. We join our hands together and say Nah-mah-skar, which means, *I greet you from within my soul* or, *You and I are one.*

Nepal is a small country (as big as Arkansas in the United States). The people of Nepal are referred to as either Nepalese or Nepali. When it is morning time in America, it is evening in Nepal. The country is famous for its mountains, wildlife, and breathtaking scenery.

Life is not easy for Nepali people, particularly in the mountain regions. Many people have to walk miles for everyday activities, like going to school or finding supplies for their families. Nepali people value family life and most live with their parents and grandparents. Rice is a staple food in the diet of most Nepalis and is eaten a few times a day, often accompanied by lentils (daal) and vegetables (tarkaari).

The country's population is diverse. Nepali is the official language, and English is the second language. The two major religions, Hinduism and Buddhism, are practiced side by side. It is common to see a Hindu temple adjacent to a Buddhist stupa in perfect harmony. The most celebrated holidays in Nepal are Dashain and Deepavali/ Tihar (Hindu holidays) and Buddha Jayanti (Buddhist holiday). Since the lunar calendar is observed, holidays do not fall on the same day every year. Nepalese people are peace loving and worship "Mother Earth", and there are special days to honor brothers and sisters, dogs, cows, birds, and even plants. Nepal is the only country in the world to have a living goddess: she is known as Kumari.

Nepalese are happy and friendly people; their hospitality is what attracts countless tourists from all over the world to this unique country, again and again! I hope you enjoy sharing this book with the children in your life.

"Namaskar"
-Anita Adhikary

To Mr. Satya Narayan B. Shrestha, a founding father of numerous educational institutions in Nepal. You inspired me from the beginning!

To Sister Anthonita Porta, without whom I may never have begun my Montessori path.

To Gaury, my ever loving husband, and my family, for always cheering me on.

Thank you to Pooja, Roshani, and Ashok for supporting me every step of the way.

And special thanks to Subi Aryal for your inspirational photographs.

Cheers,
Anita Bhandary Adhikary

N Is For Nepal

© 2011, Anita Adhikary

Requests for permission to make copies of any part of the work should be submitted online at info@mascotbooks.com or mailed to Mascot Books 560 Herndon Parkway #120, Herndon, VA 20170

Printed in the United States.

PRT0611A

ISBN-13: 978-1-936319-52-7
ISBN-10: 1-936319-52-7

Mascot Books
560 Herndon Parkway #120, Herndon, VA 20170

www.mascotbooks.com

N is for Nepal

Anita Adhikary
illustrated by
Jen Mundy

A is for Annapurna

People come from all over the world to view and climb Nepal's Annapurna Range. Trekkers call it ABC - Annapurna Base Camp.

B is for Bridges

Bridges in Nepal span running waters and gorges. They come in many forms - short, long, and narrow!

C is for Cows

Cows are worshipped in the Hindu faith. They are found everywhere - even on the streets!

D is for Dogs

Dogs are adorned with garland and given special treats on a special holiday in Nepal.

E is for Everest

Part of the Himalayas, Mt. Everest is the highest peak in the world. It stands 29,035 feet and was formed over 60 million years ago!

F is for Flag

Nepal has the only national flag that is made from two triangles. They represent mountain peaks!

G is for Gorges

Deep gorges are found all over the Nepali terrain. The most popular gorge is called *David's Fall* in Pokhara.

H is for Himalayas

The Himalayas are the majestic mountains of South Asia. Nepal boasts eight of the Himalaya's highest peaks.

I is for India

India is Nepal's neighbor to the south. The two countries share an open border spanning over 1,000 miles.

J is for Jungles

Nepali jungles are a haven for many unique animals, birds, and exotic plants.

K is for Kathmandu

Kathmandu gets its name from a temple built out of a single tree. *Kath* means wood, and *mandap* means temple. Kathmandu is Nepal's capital city.

L is for Lumbini

Located in southern Nepal, Lumbini is the birthplace of Siddhartha Gautama Buddha.

 **is for
Monkeys**

Monkeys are often seen in
Nepali temples, waiting to
grab baskets of offerings.

N is for Nepal

Nepal is a land-locked country in South Asia. To the north is Tibet and to the south is India.

O is for Outdoors

Since the weather is pleasant in most areas of Nepal, people enjoy spending time outdoors throughout the year.

P is for Pashupatinath Temple

Hindus flock to this temple of
Lord Shiva, located in Kathmandu,
on the banks of the Bagmati River.

Q is for Quails

One of the rarest birds in the world, a small number of the Himalayan Quail live in western Nepal.

R is for Rhinoceros

There are nearly five hundred one-horned rhinos living in conservation areas in Nepal.

S is for Stupas

A stupa is a place of Buddhist worship. The most famous stupas in Nepal are Swayambhunath and Boudhanath.

T is for Terai

Tigers are found primarily in Nepal's Chitwan National Park, located in the country's Terai region.

U is for Uniforms

It is customary for students to wear uniforms to school in Nepal.

V is for Vehicles

Many types of vehicles are used to transport Nepalis from one place to another.

W is for Walking

Because of the challenging terrain, Nepali people often walk to their schools and jobs.

 **X** **is for Xylography**

Xylography is the art of making wood structures. Exquisite wood carvings are seen throughout the temples of Nepal.

Y is for Yak and Yeti

Yaks live in high elevation areas. A Yeti is a mythical creature rumored to live in the Himalayas. Wouldn't it be great to see a Yeti ride on a Yak?

Z is for Zoo

There is only one zoo in
Nepal. It is in Kathmandu -
and a must see for all!

Namaskar!

About the Author

Anita B. Adhikary was born in Kathmandu, Nepal. She is a genuine citizen of the world, living in several continents and experiencing multiculturalism firsthand from a young age. Her passion is learning about other cultures and meeting people.

Mrs. Adhikary is actively involved in fundraising for great causes pertaining to the Nepali diaspora, including the Association of Nepalese in Midwest America, and the America Nepal Medical Foundation. She has co-authored a booklet for new Nepali immigrants to assist with their transition to American society.

Mrs. Adhikary has been an educator for nearly three decades, spanning from pre-school to secondary education; however, her niche has always been working with the incredibly young, in a Montessori setting. Children are her constant source of inspiration.

Mrs. Adhikary has two daughters and lives in Ann Arbor, Michigan with her husband, cat, and dog.